THE MEMORY OF JUSTICE

MICHAEL KINGSWOOD

When Jacob wakes to find himself bound to a chair in an unfamiliar room, he fears the worst.

What he discovers in that room will put his worst fears to shame.

The Memory Of Justice is a 3,000 word science fiction mystery.

———

Enjoy the book! After you're done, please come to Michael's website and sign up for his mailing list at http://www.michaelkingswood.com/newsletter-signup/. Guaranteed to be spam free, he uses it to announce new releases and special promotions for his fans.

The world was a blur of shadows and splotches of color that swirled around as Jacob turned his head from side to side. After a while, its lack of cohesion just added to the ache in his temples, turning a dull throb into stabbing pain that made him grit his teeth to hold back a groan.

At least he had teeth; a strangely comforting bit of normalcy, that.

Jacob tried to rub his brow but found his hands were restrained. He could not move them from his sides. After a moment's concentration, he realized they were resting on thin pieces of a grainy material - wood? Pressure on his back and bottom came into focus then, and he realized he was sitting in a chair, with his hands on its arms.

He blinked, and the world stopped swirling so much, coming to resemble merely an amorphous blob. An improvement. Looking down, he could just barely make out the shapes of his arms and legs, and that of the chair. But he still could not move; his arms and legs must have been bound to the chair.

Where was he? How had he gotten here?

He had no idea, and no memory of anything after Clara...

The name went through his mind like a jolt of

electricity. Sudden fear swept through him, masking his earlier anxiety beneath its weight. Was she a prisoner too?

Jacob tried to call out to her, but all that came from his mouth was a rough grunt. His mouth was dry as a desert at midday, making it difficult to sound out words, and there was an awful metallic taste lingering on his palette.

He closed his mouth and worked his jaw but saliva would not come, despite the hunger pangs that he was only just beginning to recognize for what they were. How long had he been here?

The world changed.

Light, brighter than anything else had been, stabbed into his eyes, and he recoiled. As much as he was able to recoil, restrained as he was. He blinked several times in rapid succession, willing the new purple spots to clear from his vision so he could tell what was going on.

Slowly, the glare reduced, or rather his eyes adjusted to it. And as they did so, his surroundings became more clear.

The room was not large, but roomy. The walls were off-white, probably the default paint job the original builders had applied. His chair was near the center of the floor, which was hardwood but covered in a cheap rug where he sat. Mostly-empty bookshelves lined the wall to his left; to his right was a closed hardwood door that was painted blue. There were no windows. The wall in front of him was dominated by a large video display and its control terminal. The display was dark, but a small, lit LED on its lower right corner indicated its readiness.

The light that had dazzled him so came from two large directional lamps, one in either corner of the room ahead of him. Both were turned to shine directly at him. It reminded him of the interrogation rooms cliché bad guys use in bad thriller movies.

It even smelled like he imagined such places would: clean, antiseptic, with just a hint of a cleaning solution lingering in the air.

The fear did not go away; it intensified. What the hell was going on?

A soft click drew his gaze to the right, to the door.

The knob was beginning to turn. Someone was coming in.

Jacob tried to steel himself, prepare for what was to come. It was not going to be pleasant; he knew that in his gut.

Then the door opened, and his fear gave way to surprised shock as a lean woman of medium height strode into the room. She wore jeans and a loose-fitting burgundy shirt that buttoned up the front, and athletic shoes. Her hair, red-brown and pulled back into a pony tail, framed an oval face that was dominated by a slightly-too-large nose.

His shock at seeing her here, like this, almost caused him to miss the fact that she carried a semi-automatic pistol in her right hand.

"Hello Jacob," Clara said. "We have some things to discuss."

———

Jacob shut the tap and turned back to the bar, foamy mug in hand. Lawrence waited on his usual stool, with the same expectant expression on his face as he always did. When Jacob slid the mug across to him, he grinned - again, the same lopsided grin as always - and waved his hand over the payment processing sensor. Jacob did not need to look to see how much of a tip Lawrence had left; that was always the same as well. Hell, if the man did not occasionally change ties, Jacob would be unable to tell whether he had ever left the bar.

Jacob found it quite boring; he wondered if Lawrence did as well.

"Heard about that guy they have on trial?"

Jacob shrugged. He did not pay attention to that kind of news. Too depressing. Besides, Lawrence was just going to tell him about it anyway.

To pass the time, Jacob fished a rag out of the sink next to the taps and began wiping the bar down. The darkly stained wood got dusty or stained from spilled drinks or glasses without coasters if he did not wipe it down a couple times a shift, and the owner hated that.

Not that there was much concern of spilled drinks tonight; it was Tuesday, and the place was empty except for Lawrence.

"Legal expert on the News thinks sure the jury's gonna decide guilty." Lawrence swallowed a gulp of his beer and burped softly before continuing. "Says the DA is pushing for a total memory wipe."

"That right."

Lawrence nodded, his head resembling a bobble-head doll for a moment. This was his last drink for the night. He would bitch about it, but the last thing Jacob needed was to clean up more barf.

"Not sure what I think of that." Lawrence looked down into his mug for a long moment. "It'd almost be more humane just to shoot him, you know?"

Right. Gun him down like a rabid dog. Real humane.

"Lawrence, I think you've had..."

The door swung open, drawing his gaze away from a stain that had somehow escaped his earlier wiping. When he saw the woman entering, he lost track of what she was about to say.

She glanced over at Lawrence, but quickly dismissed him, instead focusing on Jacob. Her eyes, green he thought, flickered up and down, taking him in, or as much of him as was visible above the bar anyway, and her lips turned upward into a small smile that made her face light up.

"You still serving dinner?"

"The kitchen just closed," Jacob said. Her smile faded as quickly as it appeared. He added, "But I think I can rustle something up."

She sidled up to a stool at the far end of the bar from Lawrence. "Thanks. I'm starving, and I need a beer."

"That's what I'm here for. I'm Jacob."

The woman took his hand in a gentle, but strong, grip and smiled more broadly. "Clara. Clara Cumberland."

———

"Clara, what...?"

She made a soft tsking noise. Moving with the languid grace he had admired from the first time he met her, six weeks before when she first walked into the bar, she stepped in front of his chair and leaned forward until her face was at eye level with him.

Those deep green eyes, which always before had flashed with humor and warmth, were cold, sharp.

"Shh, pigeon," she said, and he felt something cold and hard touch his left cheek. "Things will become," the hard metal of the pistol's front sight traced a line down his cheek, then across his chin as she spoke, "very clear soon enough." She smiled then, a mirthless grin that only enhanced the ice in her gaze, and stepped back from him.

He imagined he could still feel the touch of the gun against his skin as she crossed her arms and turned away, toward the display control station. What was she playing at?

"You do not remember when we first met." She spoke without turning around, instead tapping the control station to bring it to life.

"Sure I do. You had just finished unpacking and came in for dinner and a beer because you didn't feel like..."

"*No!*"

Clara rounded on him, her eyes flashing angrily for a second before she schooled her face to calm ice one more. She took a deep breath, then spoke again, more calmly.

"We did not meet six weeks ago, pigeon. You don't remember our first meeting, but I will never forget." She lowered her gaze and took another deep breath, and it was obvious Clara was forcing down some deep emotions.

What was she talking about? Jacob had never seen her before that night in the bar, he was sure of it. He opened his mouth to retort, but found the words frozen in his mouth as Clara looked back up, her frosty eyes meeting his in a gaze he could not look away from, and spoke again.

"Five years ago today, you raped and murdered my sister."

———

Stunned, Jacob just stared at Clara for what seemed an hour but in fact was probably more like thirty seconds. He had done *what*? How could she think him capable of such a thing? In his entire life, he had never laid hands on a woman, even those who really needed to be slapped or otherwise stopped from hurting themselves or others, namely him.

When he was little - three, maybe four - Jacob got into a fight with his sister, God rest her soul, and kicked her. His father had taken his belt to Jacob's bottom, then explained the reality of life in no uncertain terms. A boy - a man - does not strike, or in any way harm, a girl. Ever. For any reason.

No matter what.

"Clara, you have me confused with someone else. I've never..."

Instead of replying, Clara tapped the remote control - he had not noticed that she picked it up - and the wall display lit up.

A news broadcast began to play. It was five years old from the time stamp on the lower left corner of the screen. It showed a body being rolled into an ambulance. The entire scene was blocked off by yellow crime scene tape, and uniformed policemen stood watch all around. The title at the bottom of the screen, next to the network identification, read, "Brutal Murder in Palm Springs."

"The victim, as yet unidentified," said the off-screen anchor in a deep, professionally neutral baritone, "was found naked and beaten by a local man, who called the authorities immediately. She was pronounced dead at the scene. Police suspect she was sexually assaulted, and are beginning a canvas of the surrounding neighborhoods."

A brief flash of the victim's face appeared before the paramedics closed the ambulance doors. Young. Pretty. Though it was hard to be sure from all the bruising on her face from where her assailant had beaten her.

Jacob felt a surge of revulsion, followed be righteous indignation. What sort of a man would do that to a woman?

And how could Clara think *he* was to blame?

Jacob turned his gaze back to Clara and found her watching him with a knowing smirk.

"Repulsed? Shocked that something so horrible could happen and that I could blame you?"

He nodded.

She tapped the remote control again, and the display shifted.

Another news stream, this one dated three weeks after the first. The reporter, an olive-skinned woman with wavy black hair who wore a navy blue pants suit, stood in front of an official-looking building that was fronted by wide stairs and fluted columns. She spoke into a small microphone with practiced neutrality, though her eyes flashed - with satisfaction? - as she spoke.

"Breaking news about the serial killer that has been plaguing Palm Springs. Police today arrested a suspect in connection with the case. His identity has not been released, but officials say there is ample evidence to show that he stalked, raped, and then killed all seven victims."

Seven? Jacob shook his head and opened his mouth to speak, but the display shifted again and he lost his breath, and his stream of thought, in a heartbeat.

The video was from three days later.

"Donald Weatherby, the suspect in the Palm Springs killings, was denied bail today. The judge cited the extreme nature of the crimes and Weatherby's dismissive attitude in his decision. Weatherby was upbeat after the hearing."

"What do I care? I'll be out before long anyway," said another voice, one that sent shivers down Jacob's spine.

He wanted to look away, but he could not. He knew that voice; had known it his entire life.

He could have drawn the face of the smiling, joking man in correction-facility orange from memory.

The face was his own.

———

"What?" Jacob shook his head. "How?"

He did not do that. He could not have. And yet...

And yet there he was, plain as day.

"It's a trick. You..." He swallowed. "You doctored the video."

Clara shook her head slowly, her lips twisted into a little sneer of sadistic enjoyment, but she said nothing.

"Well that's not me!"

His shout evoked only another tap of her finger against the remote control.

The same female reporter from the earlier clip appeared on the display. This time she wore a loose-fitting blue dress that was elegant in its simplicity. In counterpoint to the neutral professionalism that Jacob had always heard reporters claim they had, she wore a broad smile and her eyes sparkled with...triumph?

"The jury has just announced its verdict in the Donald Weatherby trial, and it is unanimous: guilty on all counts. Sentencing is in two weeks. The District Attorney has announced he will push for a total memory wipe. The defense declined to comment."

The clip ended.

Jacob understood.

Oh God, it was true. He did not remember doing or saying any of those things because...

"It'd almost be more humane just to shoot him, you know?"

Lawrence's words, spoken all those weeks ago on the night Jacob and Clara first met - this time, anyway - rang in Jacob's ears. Or was it Donald? He still thought of himself as Jacob, but that was a lie, wasn't it? All his memories...what was real and what was a lie? How long had he really been here, living this life? Five years? No, the final clip had been from a year after his arrest. Four then? Two?

How long does it take to erase a man and create a new one within his own head?

He shook his head, part of himself trying to deny what was happening, but he could not. Oh Lord...he was a monster, and Lawrence was right. It would have been better if they had just put him down, all those years ago.

He was crying; he had not realized it before now, but his cheeks were wet with tears. His chest heaved and he felt the sobs wracking his chest, but it was almost as though it was another man doing it, not he.

And it really was another man, wasn't it?

Clara touched the remote control again, and a stream of pictures began flowing across the display. A young woman. Pretty, smiling, her auburn hair parted above her brows and hanging past her shoulders. Her hair done up in a bun. Cut short. Wearing a flowery summer dress. A graduation gown and cap. A bridesmaid's dress.

Jacob did not have to ask; it was Clara's sister. What was her name? He should know it...

A final picture. The young woman, her face bruised, her nose broken, several teeth missing, her eyes open in the unfocused stare of death.

Jacob gagged and looked away, trying to keep his stomach contents down.

Clara bounded across the room and grabbed him by the hair. "Look at her," she growled, and forced his head around to face the display again.

Tears streamed down his cheeks again, and he sobbed.

"I'm..."

"*What?*"

Jacob swallowed and forced the sobs down. He opened his mouth, but all that came out was a whisper. "I'm sorry."

Clara released him, more like flung him away, and stepped back two paces. Her breathing was slow, steady, but her nostrils flared like a raging beast and there was a dreadful heat in her gaze.

"You're sorry." Her voice was flat, almost dead.

She paused for a short moment, then shook her head. "Not good enough."

In the silence that followed, Jacob could clearly see, despite the ruined state of her face on the display, the family resemblance between Clara and her sister. It was an eery juxtaposition: Clara's life and vibrance next to her sister's silence and stillness. Jacob found he could not look away from the pair of them.

"What do you want from me?" He knew the answer, but he needed to hear her say it.

"They decided to wipe your memory, put in another. Send you to the other side of the world, where know one would know you, leave you here." Her sneer became a snarl. "My sister is dead, and you go on living as though nothing happened. And they call that justice."

She drew in a deep breath, then raised her right hand. Jacob had not even noticed she was still carrying the pistol.

"What do I want?" Clara said. "I want justice."

He should have been afraid. He should have cried out against the injustice of it all. But that would have been a lie. All he felt was resignation and somehow, perversely, relief. Lawrence was right, after all. All the same, he had to try.

"You know they'll catch you. Do the same as me. You won't remember her, me, you." He made a little gesture with his bound hands, taking in the room. "You won't even remember this. So what's the point?"

Clara stared at him for several seconds, then glanced off to her right. He turned his head and saw, over in the corner beside the directional lamp, a small camera. A red blinking light near its lens indicated it was recording.

"I'll remember," she said.

Then there was a flash, followed by the blackest darkness.

Thank you for reading my book. I hope you enjoyed reading it as much as I enjoyed writing it.

Every review helps an author out, so whether you loved this book, hated it, or something in between, please take a minute to tell other readers what you thought. All of the online retailers make it very easy to do, and I would really appreciate it.

Feel free to come say hi at my website or on Facebook. I always enjoy hearing from readers, especially since you all are, collectively, my boss.

I also have a weekly podcast, Story Time With Michael Kingswood, where I read stories and talk through some of the latest goings on in my world. I'd love to see you there.

Thanks again. My best to you and yours.

Warm Regards,
Michael Kingswood

MAILING LIST

If you enjoyed this book and would like word on new releases and special deals from Michael Kingswood, sign up for his newsletter on his website. Guaranteed to be spam-free, you can opt out at any time. And you can rest assured he will not share your information with anyone, for any reason.

https://michaelkingswood.com/newsletter-signup/

SUPPORTING PATRONAGE

Michael would like to invite you to become a supporting member of his website. Similar in concept to Patreon, a few dollars a month will give you access to exclusive content, and help him to focus more of his time to writing fun and exciting stories for your enjoyment.

Sign up at his website:

https://www.michaelkingswood.com/membership/
supporting-patronage/

ABOUT THE AUTHOR

Michael Kingswood is 20-year veteran of the US Navy submarine force and a lifelong fan of science fiction and fantasy literature. His work has appeared in numerous collections and anthologies, to include the Fiction River Anthology series from WMG publishing. He holds a bachelors degree in Mechanical Engineering as well as a Master of Engineering Management and a Master of Business Administration. He has four children and currently resides in San Diego.

Find Michael Kingswood online at:

www.michaelkingswood.com

www.facebook.com/michael.kingswood

steemit.com/@michaelkingswood

MORE BOOKS BY MICHAEL KINGSWOOD

GLIMMER VALE CHRONICLES

Glimmer Vale

Out-Dweller

Tollard's Peak

Robbed Blind

Wedding Gifts: A Glimmer Vale Chronicles Story

The Falconer's Stairs

Glimmer Vale Omnibus Edition #1

———

THE PERICLES CONSPIRACY

Passing In The Night

The Pericles Conspiracy

———

DAWN OF ENLIGHTENMENT

Masters Of The Sun

———

NOVELLAS

What Lurks Between

The Necromancer's Lair

The Champion

Veritas Morte

STORY COLLECTIONS

Tales Of Adventure #1

Tales Of Adventure #2

Short Story 10-Pack

A Jar Of Mixed Treats

SHORT FICTION

Michael has also published a number of shorter works, links
to which can be found on his website.

www.ingramcontent.com/pod-product-compliance
Lightning Source LLC
Chambersburg PA
CBHW032054180726
48284CB00004B/1341